Where on earth would you go in a magic camper?

✪

"I'd go to the beaches of Hawaii, collect shells, and play in the ocean all day." —Eli

"I would go to the Amazon rain forest." —Haley

"I'd go to Uranus. But before I left Earth, I'd go to the park." —Theo

"Florida because my grandparents are there." —Gus

"Either Long Beach Island, New Jersey, or Pittsburgh. I can't decide." —Eleanor

Travel with
Finn and Molly in

MAGIC ON THE MAP ①
LET'S MOOOVE!

COURTNEY SHEINMEL & BIANCA TURETSKY
illustrated by STEVIE LEWIS

A STEPPING STONE BOOK™
Random House 🏠 New York

For Jo...

For L...

—B.T.

Text copyright © 2019 by Courtney Sheinmel and Bianca Turetsky
Cover art and interior illustrations copyright © 2019 by Stevie Lewis

All rights reserved. Published in the United States by Random House Children's
Books, a division of Penguin Random House LLC, New York.

Random House and the colophon are registered trademarks and
A Stepping Stone Book and the colophon are trademarks of
Penguin Random House LLC.

Visit us on the Web! rhcbooks.com

Educators and librarians, for a variety of teaching tools, visit us at
RHTeachersLibrarians.com

Library of Congress Cataloging-in-Publication Data
Names: Sheinmel, Courtney, author. | Turetsky, Bianca, author. |
Lewis, Stevie, illustrator.
Title: Let's mooove! / Courtney Sheinmel and Bianca Turetsky;
illustrated by Stevie Lewis.
Other titles: Let us mooove! | Let's move!
Description: New York: Random House, [2019] | Series: Magic on the map; #1 |
"A Stepping Stone Book." | Summary: On the last day of second grade, twins
Finn and Molly discover a magical camper in their driveway that takes them
from Ohio to Colorado, where they must save a famous cow.
Identifiers: LCCN 2018035403 | ISBN 978-1-63565-166-9 (trade) |
ISBN 978-1-63565-167-6 (lib. bdg.) | ISBN 978-1-63565-168-3 (ebook)
Subjects: | CYAC: Cattle stealing—Fiction. | Recreational vehicles—Fiction. |
Magic—Fiction. | Brothers and sisters—Fiction. | Twins—Fiction. |
Colorado—Fiction.
Classification: LCC PZ7.S54124 Let 2019 | DDC [Fic]—dc23

Printed in the United States of America
10 9 8 7 6 5 4 3 2 1

This book has been officially leveled by using the F&P Text Level Gradient™
Leveling System.

Random House Children's Books supports the First Amendment

Contents

Chapter One

DRIVEWAY SURPRISE

On the last day of second grade, Finn and Molly Parker came home to find a camper in their driveway. It was white with one orange stripe and one yellow stripe. It had a rounded roof and three windows on the sides.

The twins checked to make sure the school bus had let them off at the right house. Yep. This was 24 Birchwood Drive. With its

hunter-green mailbox out front and purple Johnny-jump-up flowers in the window
boxes. But you couldn't see the window boxes
now. They were blocked by the camper, which
was as big as a boat!

Molly turned to Finn. "What's
this doing here?" she asked.

"How would I know?" Finn asked. "I just got here, same as you."

Molly and Finn walked up the driveway slowly and carefully, as if the camper were a UFO. Finn was wearing his favorite baseball cap. It was from his Little League team, the Moonwalkers, and he never took it off.

Well, not *never*. He took it off at school because hats were not allowed during class. And he took it off each night when he had to shower before bed. But every other minute of the day, he wore it, even when he was sleeping.

Except right now, he took the hat off and shielded his eyes with his hand, peeking through the camper's tinted windows.

Their dad jumped out of the driver's side door.

"AH!" the twins yelled in surprise.

"Dad, you scared us," Finn said. "What are you doing home?"

"And what's *this*?" Molly added.

"It's a camper! Isn't it beautiful?" Mr. Parker said. He patted the side of the camper as if it were a new puppy. "Now we can take the trip I've always dreamed of taking."

"What trip?" Finn asked.

"A family road trip!" their dad exclaimed. "We can go anywhere our hearts desire."

"That's not true. We can't go to Bora Bora," Molly said.

"Huh?" Finn asked.

"Bora Bora is an island in Tahiti," Molly said. "It's in the middle of the Pacific Ocean, which means we can't drive there. Anywhere we travel in the camper has to be on this continent."

"That's right, Mol," their dad said. "Can't get anything past you! But there are lots of other places these wheels can take us this summer! We can go anywhere in North America. Doesn't that sound great?"

"I get carsick," Molly said. "Remember the time we drove to Grandma's house and I threw up all over Finn?"

"*I* remember," Finn said. "It was so disgusting!"

"I didn't do it on purpose," Molly replied.

"But you didn't have to do it on *me*," Finn said. "Do you get camper-sick, too?"

"Probably," Molly said.

"Gross," Finn said, placing his cap back on his head.

"Kids, where's that Parker family spirit?" their dad asked.

Just then, Mrs. Parker stepped out of the front door, her cell phone pressed to her ear. Her eyes widened at the sight of a camper in her driveway. "Carol, I'm going to have to call you back," she said. She lowered the phone and shook her head. "What in the world ...?"

"Family vacation, honey!" Mr. Parker said.

Mrs. Parker's eyes scanned the driveway. "Where's your car?"

"I traded with Professor Vega in the astrophysics department!" Mr. Parker exclaimed. "It was a steal of a deal! The car only sat five, and this camper sleeps eight!"

"Oh no," Mrs. Parker said. "You have to trade back. This takes up the entire front yard. And it's crushing my poor marigolds!"

"Phew," Molly and Finn sighed with relief.

The camper would be returned tomorrow.

Dad would get his regular old car back. Everything would be normal again.

But that night, Molly couldn't fall asleep. She tossed and turned until there was a faint morning light peeking through her window shade.

Molly put on her fuzzy bunny slippers and carefully tiptoed down the stairs. She wanted to look at the camper one last time, and maybe go inside it before Dad traded it back. She couldn't get carsick (or *camper*-sick) if it was standing still.

She quietly slipped outside and opened the unlocked camper door. To her surprise, someone was already there.

Chapter Two

MAGIC CAMPER

Finn was in the back of the camper, dressed in his gray-and-blue pajamas, matching slippers, and, of course, his baseball cap.

"What are you doing here?" Molly and Finn asked at the same time.

Molly was going to say, "jinx," but then Finn wouldn't be allowed to talk, and she really did want to know the answer.

"I've never been inside a camper before,"

Finn said. "I just wanted to see what it was like."

"Yeah," Molly said. "Me too."

The twins didn't look much alike. Molly's long hair was reddish-brown and wavy. Her eyes were the color of chocolate Milk Duds, just like their dad's. Finn had hair the color of dark chocolate, and it was clipped so short you couldn't tell if it was straight or curly. His eyes were as blue as the ocean, just like their mom's. But even though Finn and Molly looked different, and even though they liked different things, sometimes they were thinking the exact same thing at the exact same time. That was the case right now.

"Do you know what I'm thinking?" Finn asked his sister.

She nodded. "You're thinking we should explore this thing."

They walked the length of the main room of the camper. It was a kitchen, a dining room, and a bedroom all rolled into one. The furniture was squished close together and bolted to the wall. "I bet they did that so it doesn't slide around when the camper is moving," Molly said.

"I knew that," Finn told her. He pulled a lever on the couch and it turned into a bed. The counter turned into a table. The cabinet turned into a TV.

"Everything has to be two-in-one because there's not enough room for stuff to just be what it is," Molly added. "The camper is bigger than a car but smaller than a house."

"I knew that, too," Finn replied.

In the very back of the camper, there was a bathroom the size of a tiny closet. Outside the bathroom, just above the sink, a bulletin board was bolted to the wall. A map of the world had been pinned up, just like the one in Ms. Gitty's second-grade classroom. Molly undid the safety lock on the cabinet beneath the sink and found a container of

multicolored pushpins. She took a red pin and pushed it right into where their town was on the map. Harvey Falls, Ohio. She and Finn had lived there all their lives.

"You shouldn't do that," Finn told her. "It's not our property. At least, it won't be as soon as Dad trades it back for the car."

"I want the next people to know we were here," Molly explained. She stared at her home state of Ohio. Her house and her town and her state had always seemed rather big to Molly. But on this world map, her state was the size of a wad of gum, her town was the size of a pinprick, and her house was too small to be on the map at all. Molly sighed.

"What's wrong?" her brother asked.

"It looks lonely," she said.

"The pushpin?" he asked.

"Yes." Molly sighed again.

"You're being ridiculous," Finn told her. "Pushpins aren't alive. They don't get lonely."

Molly knew that her brother was right. Besides, it was probably time to go back to bed anyway.

But Finn had moved to the front of the camper, where there were two big leather seats. One was the passenger seat and one was the driver's seat. Finn had never sat in the driver's seat before, but now was his chance to try. He sat down and put his hands on the steering wheel. His legs were too short to reach the pedals.

"Where to?" he called back to his sister. "If we go east, we could go to … to … what state is east again? I can't remember."

Molly sat down in the passenger seat and

rolled her eyes. "Pennsylvania," she said. "Didn't you pay attention to *anything* Ms. Gitty said?"

Finn shrugged. It was hard to pay attention in class sometimes, especially during baseball season. "Or we could go west," he said. "To whatever state that is." He twisted the wheel right and left. "Or we could go to France!"

"France is another country," Molly told her brother. "On a different continent."

"Fine. We could go up to Canada, though. That's our continent, right?"

Molly nodded. "Up north."

"Or we could go way, way, *waaaaay* down, all the way to Mexico!" Finn said. "Vroom! *Vroooooom!*"

"You shouldn't be playing around like

that," Molly told her brother. "Mom and Dad always say cars aren't toys. A camper isn't, either!"

"Relax," Finn said. "We don't have any keys. We can't really go anywhere."

He twisted the wheel some more. Molly fingered the blue-and-purple friendship bracelet on her wrist. That's what she did when she was nervous. She'd made the bracelet herself, and she wanted to give it to a friend. She just hadn't decided who that would be yet.

Finn pressed the button next to the steering wheel to turn on the radio, but nothing happened. "I wish we *did* have the keys," he said. "It's much more fun to pretend-drive when you have music to sing along to."

He began to sing his favorite song out

loud: "Take me out to the ball game, take me out with the crowd ..."

Molly examined the little TV screen in the middle of the dashboard. There were also red buttons labeled POWER and VOLUME, plus up and down arrows in blue.

"It's weird that there's a TV up here," Molly said. "Drivers shouldn't watch TV. It's unsafe." She pressed the POWER button, even though she knew that it wouldn't work without the keys to turn the camper on.

But the strangest thing happened. The TV screen lit up, first a flash of white, then blue, and finally the word WELCOME popped up on the screen, each letter in bright red.

A deep voice came out of the speaker. "Hello," it said. "Who are you?"

Chapter Three

BUCKLE UP
AND DON'T PUKE

Finn almost fell out of his seat, and Molly actually did fall out of hers!

"Hello," the robot-like voice called. "Hello, hello, *hellooooo?*"

Molly glanced up at her brother from the camper floor. "Finn ...," she said softly.

"Your name is Finn?" the voice asked. "Funny, you don't *sound* like a Finn."

The twins' eyes moved to the same place:

the keyhole on the right side of the steering wheel. The *empty* keyhole. Then they looked at each other. Their eyes were wide, and their mouths hung open in shock.

"How do you do, Finn?" the voice asked.

"I'm not—I'm not Finn," Molly said, climbing back into her seat. "Finn is my brother."

"Don't talk to it, Molly," Finn whispered.

"Why shouldn't she talk to me?" the voice asked.

"Because you're a camper!" Finn said. And then he clamped his mouth shut because he realized now *he* was talking to it.

"Young man," the voice said, sounding slightly insulted, "tell me something. Have you ever talked to a camper before? Has a camper ever talked to you?"

"No," Finn said. "That was my point."

"Precisely," the voice said. "That is because I am *not* a camper. I'm a Planet Earth Transporter."

"Huh?" Finn said.

"You can call me PET for short," the voice said. "I know every street, highway, parkway,

freeway, cul-de-sac, interstate, dirt road, and wooded pathway there is."

"My mom's car knows all that, too!" Molly said. "It's called GPS."

PET made a *harrumph* noise. "GPS. Big whoop. There's nothing hard about being a computer that tells the driver to use *normal* roads. Normal roads have traffic, potholes, and stoplights. Any old machine can do that," PET said. "But I travel using the internet."

"You can't *travel* on the internet," Molly said. "You can only log on to look up information."

"Why do they call it a super*highway*, then?" PET asked.

"Because—because . . . ," the twins stuttered, but neither of them knew the answer.

"I can prove it," PET said. "Just tell me where to go. Anywhere you want."

"I've always wanted to go to training camp," Finn said. "The major league baseball teams all train in Florida or Arizona, but that's in March."

"No way!" Molly said. "I'm not going to watch a bunch of boring teams in a boring game—"

"It's not boring!" Finn said.

"Well, we can't go," PET said.

"I knew it!" Molly said. She turned to Finn. "Information travels on the internet, but people don't!"

"Actually," PET said, "since spring training is in March, and it is presently June, I'm unable to take you there. I am many things, but a time machine is not one of them. Maybe

I should pick the first destination. We'll start close by, practically in your own backyard."

"Why do we need a camper to go somewhere in our backyard?" Finn muttered.

"Buckle your seat belts!" PET said.

The screen lit up. The camper started humming and shaking. Then there was a near-blinding flash of bright white light.

"Finn!" Molly shouted.

"Don't puke on me again!" Finn shouted back.

"Don't worry," PET said. "We'll be there in a jiff."

The twins gripped the armrests of their seats tightly.

"Oh no, oh no, oh no!" Molly cried.

"It's okay, Molly," Finn said, though his own voice was quivering. "I'm sure this is

some kind of joke. Or it's a dream. I'm in pajamas, and so are you." He glanced at Molly's
blue top and leggings. "And since we sometimes think the same things, maybe we could
be having the same dream and …"

But then Finn looked out the window.
He saw snow-peaked mountains and miles

of winding rivers that led to a massive lake. Farther on, he saw a forest that looked like it was made up of giant Christmas trees. There were lavender and white wildflowers everywhere. A flock of small brown birds flew by the passenger side window.

"I've never seen birds like those in our backyard before," Finn said.

"They're larks," Molly told her brother.

"You think you know everything about everything," Finn grumbled. "Even in my dreams."

The camper stopped with a jolt. Suddenly, it was still and quiet.

The twins weren't sure of many things. But one thing they knew for sure: they weren't in the driveway of 24 Birchwood Drive anymore.

Chapter Four

HOLY GUACAMOLE

For a few seconds, Molly and Finn were speechless. But PET wasn't. "I'll be back when your work here is done," it said.

And then the screen went dark. All the camper doors swung wide open.

Molly pushed the POWER button. Nothing. She pushed all the other buttons. Again and again and again. Nothing happened. Zip. Zilch. Nada.

"What should we do?" Finn asked.

"I guess we go outside and figure out what our work is," Molly said.

They walked down the camper steps and onto the dewy ground. Molly could feel her boots sinking into the wet earth.

Wait a second. *Boots?!*

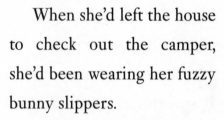

When she'd left the house to check out the camper, she'd been wearing her fuzzy bunny slippers.

"Finn!" Molly cried. "Look at what we're wearing!"

Finn's eyes widened as he took in his sister's outfit. She had on a purple-and-white gingham button-down shirt, jeans, and brown cowboy

boots. Finn was in a gray-and-blue shirt and blue jeans, which were tucked into black cowboy boots. And on his head …

Finn's hands flew to the top of his head. *Phew!* He had his Moonwalkers hat on.

But the rest of his outfit was still a problem.

"Those were my favorite pajamas!" Finn whined. "What happened to our stuff?"

"I don't know," Molly admitted.

"For once," Finn said.

There was a siren sound from Finn's back pocket, and he reached back to pull out something no bigger than a deck of cards.

"Oh, my baseball video game!" he exclaimed. "Thank goodness! I thought I lost this, too." He pressed a few buttons. "It's the seventh-inning stretch now, so I have a break.

We can get started on whatever work PET was talking about."

"You seriously need to rethink your priorities," Molly told him.

Finn turned the game off and returned it to his pocket. Molly wrapped her arms around herself. The sky was barely light, and it was much colder than it had been back home. She wished she had her fleece jacket. But she didn't know she would be somewhere that was so cold—in June!

"Holy guacamole, it's cold," Finn said, which was exactly what Molly was thinking.

The twins looked across the pasture. There was a flagpole at the far end. The flag at the top was blue-and-white-striped with a big red "C" in the center. Beyond it, the sun was coming up behind a red-roofed building.

There were two old rocking chairs out front and a trail of smoke winding from a brick chimney.

"Look at that," Molly said, pointing to a white wooden sign. "It says Snowflake Ranch Mess Hall. I guess that means we're at the Snowflake Ranch."

"Where's that?" Finn asked.

"I don't know," Molly said again. She was used to knowing things, and she did *not* like not knowing two different things in the space of five minutes.

"Well," Finn said, "I think we should go inside and find someone to help us."

Molly felt a chill. Maybe it was the sudden gust of wind. Maybe it was the new, strange feeling of not knowing. But she was scared that something bad was about to happen.

That's when the door to the mess hall burst open. A plump woman in an apron began clanging a big bell on the porch.

CLANG CLANG CLANG!

The woman spot-

32

ted Molly and Finn across the grass. "You kids here for breakfast?"

The twins looked at each other. They *were* hungry. They both nodded.

"Well, come on in! The early bird catches the worm!" She motioned for the twins to follow her inside. "I'm Helen, and I made everything myself. I don't mind saying, my food tastes so good, you'll be mopping your plates!"

Inside was a breakfast buffet that smelled of everything delicious: pancakes, home fries, bacon, cheesy eggs, and sweet Danish.

"Is this free?" Molly asked Finn.

"I don't see any prices," Finn said as he piled his plate high with all his favorite breakfast foods. He and Molly sat at the end of a wooden bench. Without talking about it, the twins made a silent agreement to eat, then ask for help. After a bite of cheesy eggs, they helped themselves to more. Pretty soon the mess hall filled up.

"What do you think of my new shirt?" a man in a red flannel shirt asked the woman next to him.

"Looks great," she told him.

"Last one in the store," he said. "It's my new favorite."

"Big day ahead," another man said. He was in a green button-down.

"Have you used the lasso yet?" asked someone else.

"Sure did," the man in the green shirt said. "Yesterday I almost caught a calf. Soon I may even be able to rope in one of those rogue cowboys."

"Did I hear you say something about the rogue cowboys?" a young girl asked. She sat down at the other end of Molly and Finn's table, balancing a plate of scrambled eggs. She had corkscrew-curly hair, and she looked about a year or two older than the twins.

Molly leaned toward her brother and whispered, " 'Rogue' means someone dangerous or dishonest."

"I knew that," Finn whispered back.

"Hey, Ella," a woman said to the girl. "These guys think two days of lassoing makes them a match for a bunch of Colorado outlaws. What do you think?"

"My dad has worked at the Snowflake Ranch since before I was born," Ella said. "He says the stories of rogue cowboys are nothing but tall tales."

"Well, there you have it," the woman said.

"I'm ready anyway," the man in the green shirt insisted. He knocked his fist on the table, which sent an open ketchup bottle flying toward the man in the new flannel shirt!

Finn was up on his knees in a flash. He dove forward and cupped his hands like he was going for a ground ball in a baseball game. He caught the bottle, turned it right side up, and placed it back on the table. Not a drop of ketchup had spilled out.

"Nice work!" the man in flannel said.

The twins looked at each other. Did he say "work"? Could that be what PET had in mind?

"Thanks for your help," the man said.

"It was nothing," Finn replied.

He and Molly finished eating. They weren't sure what to do with their empty plates, so they took them over to Helen. "Is there a sink?" Molly asked.

They had a rule at home: bring your empty plates to the sink.

Helen wiped her hands on her apron. "I'll take care of it," she said, taking Molly's plate and Finn's as well.

"Can we ask you a question?" Finn asked.

"Sure thing," Helen said. "But first I have a question for you two."

"What's that?" Molly said.

"What are your names?" Helen asked.

"I'm Finn, and this is my sister, Molly," Finn said.

"Nice to meet you, Finn and Molly. Your parents are still back in the cabins?"

"N—" Finn started.

But Molly interrupted him. "They're still

sleeping," she said. It was not really a lie, because her parents were sleeping . . . back at home, where Molly and Finn were supposed to be.

"You're not planning on going out on the trail without proper cowboy hats, are ya?" Helen asked.

"Um. No?" Finn gave his answer like he was asking a question.

"Good," she said. "Head on out and make a right. It's twenty paces to the general store. Tell Cliff that I sent you, and he'll get you outfitted. He has the best hat selection in Colorado."

Finn and Molly locked eyes.

Colorado?!

Chapter Five

THE MOST FAMOUS COW IN COLORADO

The twins walked back outside.

"Why did you interrupt me?" Finn asked his sister.

"Because we don't need help anymore," Molly replied. "You heard what the man said."

Finn looked at Molly, not remembering.

"He said 'Nice work,'" Molly reminded Finn. "That means our work here is done."

"Oh, right." Finn smiled. They could go home!

"The part I don't understand," Molly continued, "is how we can be in Colorado. It takes at least seven minutes to drive from our house to the next town over. I don't think PET was traveling that long."

"Maybe PET can go faster than a car," Finn said. "Aroldis Chapman can throw a fastball over a hundred miles an hour!"

"Who's Aroldis Chapman?" Molly asked.

"He was a pitcher for the Cincinnati Reds before he was traded to the New York Yankees," Finn said. "Duh."

"We're not talking about baseball," Molly said. "And besides, even if PET is faster than a car, there's no way we could've crossed"—she paused to count in her head—"five state borders that quickly!"

"Maybe you're wrong," Finn said. "Maybe Colorado isn't that far away. Maybe it's right next to Ohio."

"I got a hundred percent on all of our geography quizzes, remember?" Molly said. "Colorado is definitely five states from home. It's bordered by Utah, Wyoming, Nebraska, Kansas, Oklahoma, and New Mexico."

Finn lowered his head. "You sound like a textbook," he muttered. "Anyway, it doesn't matter. That man said 'Nice work.' As soon as we find PET, we can go home. Mom and Dad will be worried if they wake up and we're not there."

They crossed the pasture to where they'd

left the camper. But all they saw were tire tracks.

"PET!" they both called. The camper was nowhere in sight. The wind blew across the deserted field.

"Here, PET," Finn said. "Oh, PET. Come *heeeeeeeeere!*"

"Come on, camper, camper, camper!" Molly added. But it was no use.

"I'm still freezing," Finn said. "Maybe we should go see Cliff in the general store. I could use a new jacket."

Molly didn't have a better idea, so they headed over to the Snowflake Ranch general store. They pulled open a heavy red door that had a cattle horn as a handle.

Inside the store, there were shelves of plaid shirts and blue jeans. There was a sales counter in the back, and behind the counter, a man was dusting rows and rows of cowboy hats.

"Excuse me," Finn called.

The man turned around. "Well, howdy," he said, tipping his own cowboy hat in greeting.

"Are you Cliff?" Molly asked.

"Sure am," the man said. "I'm the owner of this here store. Have been for twenty-five years. How can I help you?"

"Helen sent us to get some hats," Molly said.

"Yeah, and I would like a jacket, too," Finn added.

"You two must be going on the cattle drive," Cliff said. "Well, let me tell you something. You make sure to keep your eye on Snowflake, you hear?"

"Snowflakes!" Finn said. "You mean it's going to be cold enough for snowflakes?"

Cliff let out a loud laugh. "Not snowflakes," he said. "*The* Snowflake. They say no snowflake is the same, and that sure is true of *our* Snowflake. She's a five-time blue-ribbon winner. You haven't lived until you've tasted the cheese made from her milk."

"We had cheesy scrambled eggs for breakfast," Molly said. "They were amazing."

"The best ever," Finn agreed.

"That's cheese from Snowflake all right," Cliff said. "Those executives from EZ Cheezy have been trying to get their hands on her for years. They want to hook her up to machines and milk her dry. But we're not sellin'. She makes just enough for those of us at the ranch to enjoy. She deserves to roam free in the mountains, not be living in some factory."

"Ah, I get it," Molly said. "Snowflake is a cow!"

"That's right," Cliff said. "Our pride and joy." He gestured to the T-shirts, mugs, and bumper stickers in the display case under the counter. Everything had a picture of a white cow on it. "She's the most famous cow in all of Colorado."

"She looks nice," Finn said. As far as he was concerned, cows weren't mean or nice. They were just cows. But he could tell Snowflake meant a lot to Cliff.

"That she is," he said. "Now, let's get on with things here."

He stepped out from behind the counter and grabbed a couple of dark-blue jean jackets from a rack. "I think these should fit."

"Thanks," Finn said.

"Wait," said Molly. "Do we need to pay for these? We didn't bring any money."

"If you're going on the cattle drive, it's all included," Cliff said. "So let's talk hats. You're going to have to pick your own. Every rancher should pick out his—or her—own hat."

Cliff's arms swept toward the rows of cowboy hats in all different colors and sizes.

Molly gasped when she spotted one that matched her friendship bracelet: a blue straw hat with a purple band around the rim. "That one," she said. "Definitely."

But Finn wasn't sure. He tried on a straw hat, a felt hat, a wide-brim hat, a ten-gallon hat. Nothing felt quite right. His worn Moon-walkers cap was like a part of his head, and he didn't want to give it up. "I think I'll hold on to my own hat," he finally decided.

"No shame in that," Cliff said. "Here are some snacks for your pack. It's gonna be a long day."

Cliff handed them a paper bag filled with

beef jerky, red and black licorice twists, and two ice-cold bottles of water.

"You don't want to be late!" Cliff said. And with that, he pushed them out the door.

Chapter Six

HOWDY, PARTNER

"Do you think our work isn't done yet?" Finn asked.

"I don't know," Molly said. There were those words again! *I don't know*. They tasted bad every time she had to say them.

"I never thought I'd say this," Finn said, "but I actually like it better when you *do* know things."

"Me too," Molly said.

"We should ask the next person we see to help us," Finn said.

"I was thinking about that," Molly said. "We could get in trouble if we tell someone what happened. We're not allowed to cross the street, and now we've crossed state lines!"

"But it's not our fault we're here!" Finn said. "We got into the camper, it started talking, and boom! We're in Colorado."

"Yeah, I know," Molly said. "But do you think Mom or Dad will believe we traveled hundreds of miles, by ourselves, in a magic camper? Besides, we weren't supposed to be in the camper at all."

"Good point," Finn said.

Across the field, Helen stepped in front of a big red barn and motioned for the kids to hurry. "C'mon over!" Helen called. "Y'all are the last to saddle up!"

Molly looked at her brother. "What should we do?"

"I guess we should saddle up," he said.

Molly and Finn ran across the tall grass. Helen slid open the barn door, and they followed her down a long, wide hall. There were horse stalls on either side.

Finn sniffed the air. "It smells like a candy shop in here," he said.

"That's sweet feed," Helen told him. "A mix of oats and molasses. It's what the residents prefer to eat."

Neigh!

Molly and Finn both jumped in surprise. Helen unlatched a stall door. Inside, there was a big brown horse with speckles of white that looked like paint splotches.

"That's all right, boy," Helen said. She led the horse out into the hall, where the twins were waiting. "Finn, this is Rocket. Rocket, this is Finn."

"Nice to meet you," Finn said.

The horse snorted in reply.

Helen pulled sugar cubes out of her pocket and handed some to Finn. "No thanks," Finn said. "We just ate."

Helen laughed. "They're not for you," she said. "They're for Rocket. Go on, hold them flat in your palm and feed him. He'll want to be your new best friend."

Finn had never had a horse for a best friend before. Rocket stomped a front hoof and neighed again, baring his teeth. Monster-sized teeth. Teeth that didn't look like they were waiting for something as small as a sugar cube. They looked like they were waiting for something bigger … like the hand of an eight-year-old boy!

Finn stepped back, and back, and back, until he was up against the stall door. Rocket moved toward him. Finn could hear his heart banging in his chest. In one swift chomp,

Rocket scooped the sugar cubes from Finn's shaking hand. The horse's lips brushed against his palm. "Wow," Finn said. "I can't believe it. I fed a horse!"

"Good job!" Helen said. "Now, Molly, let me introduce you to Dasha."

In the next stall was a black horse with a black mane. Molly held out a sugar cube on her palm. She giggled when Dasha's lips tickled her hand.

"The horses are already saddled up," Helen said. "Let's get you two riding."

"We've never been horseback riding before," Molly admitted. "I mean, I've read about it, of course, but have never actually done it."

"Don't you worry, I'll show you both the ropes," Helen said. She pushed a little stepladder up to Rocket's left side. "Finn, why don't you go first? Step up and swing your right leg over to the other side."

Finn did exactly what Helen said. He climbed the stepladder and swung his right leg over the horse's back. "Hey, Molly, look at me! I'm on a horse!"

Helen handed Finn the reins, and Finn shook them gently. Rocket took a few steps.

"Well, look at that," Helen said. "You took to riding like a horse takes to oats. Pretty soon it'll feel as natural as breathing."

"Good boy," Finn said to the horse, patting his brown-and-white coat.

Ella, the girl they'd seen at breakfast, trotted down the hall on a white horse with black speckles. "Hey!" she called to Finn. "Rocket really likes you."

"Cool," Finn said, patting Rocket's mane. "I like you, too, boy."

"Let's ride together once we get out on the trail," Ella said.

"You bet!" Finn replied. He was excited. He didn't expect to be in Colorado this morning, and he had no idea how to get home. But as long as he was here, he might as well have fun.

Molly shifted her feet uncomfortably.

"Now your turn," Helen told her. She slid the ladder over toward Dasha.

Molly looked up at the horse. She looked back at the ground. It seemed as if there was at least six feet between them.

"You're not afraid of heights?" she asked Finn.

"Nah," he said. "It's just like jumping to catch a fly ball."

"I've never caught a fly ball," Molly reminded him.

"But you've seen me do it plenty of times."

All right, Molly thought. *If Finn can do it, then I can do it.*

She stepped on the ladder, took a deep breath, and leapt up. But instead of landing on Dasha's back, she went tumbling to the ground as the ladder slipped out from under her.

"Neigh!" Dasha called.

Molly had fallen into a pile of hay.

"When a cowgirl falls, it's important to get back on the horse," Helen said. "Unless you land on a cactus, in which case you may want to scream in pain for a little while. But no cacti here. Let me give you a hand."

She pulled Molly back up to her feet.

"Thanks," said Molly.

Helen locked her hands together. "Give me your left foot, and I'll hoist you up."

With a big boost, Molly finally landed in the saddle. It didn't feel so bad. In fact, it was kind of cool. Molly twisted around to tell Finn, but when she did, she accidentally kicked Dasha in the side with her boot.

Dasha took off at a gallop. She bolted out the barn door with Molly on her back.

Molly could hear Finn calling her name. Helen was shouting, "Pull back! Pull back!"

But Molly could only hold on to the reins with all her might. Dasha kept on running, past a crowd of people, a few horses, and so many cows! There was no sign of slowing down.

Molly squeezed her eyes
shut. She was too scared to see
what would happen next. Would she crash?
Would she *die*?

She didn't see the hand that reached out
and grabbed the reins. But she felt herself
slowing down. Carefully, she opened one eye,
then the other. Right beside her and Dasha
was another horse and rider, and that rider
now had Dasha's reins in his hands.

"Whoa, girl. Easy," the rider said, giving the reins a last, strong tug.

Dasha quickly stopped, and Molly had to hang on to the horse's neck so she didn't fly over her head.

"Howdy, partner," the man said. "I'm Roger. I'll be leading the cattle drive to Black Mountain. And who are you, tenderfoot?"

"What?" Molly asked, breathless.

"That's cowboy speak for a new person," Roger said. "What's your name?"

"Molly," she said. Her heart was still pounding.

Finn and Rocket trotted up beside Molly. Finn thought her face looked as white as a brand-new baseball. "Are you okay?" he asked.

"I don't know," Molly said.

"Riding a horse is just like riding a bike,"

Roger said. "If you fall off, you have to get right back on again."

Her heartbeat slowed down. She could do this. "Okay," Molly said.

"Think you're ready to go on a cattle drive?" Roger asked.

Molly nodded. "Yeah."

"Me too," Finn said.

Roger waved his hat in the air and cried, "YEEHAW!"

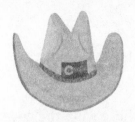

Chapter Seven
THE WEIRDEST DAY

Being outside in Colorado was different from being outside in Ohio. There were no paved streets, only miles of emerald-green grass. From on top of their horses, the twins looked out over the wilderness. Red jagged rocks sprouted up from the ground. Snow-topped mountains could be seen in the distance.

All the people who'd been in the mess hall

at breakfast, plus Roger, were on horseback in front of them.

And then there were the cows: White cows with black splotches, brown cows with white patches, big cows, baby cows. It was like an endless sea. But instead of water, there were cows, cows, and more cows. Finn had tried to count them, but it was impossible to keep track of them all when they were moving. His best guess was at least five hundred cows.

"Look at that!" Finn called to his sister, pointing to one cow that didn't look like any of the others. She was white with no splotches. A couple of ranch hands were riding their horses beside her. "That must be Snowflake!"

"She's beautiful," Molly said. "I mean, beautiful for a cow."

"Beautiful for a cow," Finn repeated.

"That's so weird. And you know what else is weird?"

"What?" Molly asked.

"We're riding horses next to cows," said Finn. "This is the weirdest day of my life!"

"Mine too," Molly said. "And Mom and Dad don't even know we're here. Do you think they're awake by now?"

"Probably," Finn replied. "They must be really mad."

"They must be really scared," said Molly. "I hope our work is done soon so we can get home."

Roger turned to look over his shoulder. "Great job keeping up the rear!" he called.

"'Job,'" Molly repeated. "That's another word for 'work.'"

"Do you think this is the work PET was talking about?" Finn asked. "To follow a bunch of cows on horseback?"

"Maybe," Molly said. She patted Dasha's soft neck. "I wish PET had been more specific."

Ella circled back and steered her horse in between Rocket and Dasha. "Where are you from?" she asked.

"Harvey Falls, Ohio," Finn answered. "What about you?"

"I live here," Ella said.

"You do?" Molly asked.

"Well, actually, I split my time between the Snowflake Ranch, where my dad lives, and Orlando, where my mom lives."

"Who's your dad?" Finn asked.

"That's him," Ella said. She pointed to Roger! "I spend every summer here with him. During the school year, I live in Orlando with my mom."

"Orlando is in Florida, by the way," Molly told her brother. "It's where Disney World is. But Orlando isn't the capital. That's Tallahassee, and Denver is the capital of Colorado."

"Do you know you sound like a textbook again?" Finn asked.

Molly sighed. Then Dasha sped up, and Molly's hands clutched the reins tighter.

"I wouldn't mind being in Disney World right now," she said. "I bet the rides there aren't as scary as this!"

"Oh, the horseback rides here are way better," Ella said. "You don't have to wait in long lines to go on them. And each time it's a whole new adventure."

Dasha neighed as if she was agreeing. Molly gripped the reins even tighter.

"What are all the cows for?" Finn asked.

"We're leading the cows," Ella explained. "That's why we're on horseback."

"Leading them where?" Molly asked.

"To their pasture, so they can graze," Ella answered.

"The cows don't know how to get there themselves?" asked Finn.

"No," Ella said. "But cows are awesome

in lots of other ways. They have really strong senses of smell, and they're extremely curious. If we weren't leading them right now, they'd probably wander off to check out that clover field. I bet they can smell the clover from here!"

"So we ride with the cows," Finn said. "Is that all we do?"

"We also have campfires and white-water rafting," said Ella. "And a square dance!"

"A square dance?" Molly asked. "What's that?"

"It's the state—" Ella began.

But Finn interrupted her. "What's that noise?"

"What noise?" Ella and Molly asked.

"That one," Finn said. "Shh." The girls listened. In the distance they could make out a steady knocking sound. It came from above them, in the trees. The knocking sound got faster and faster. "Is it . . . ?"

"Is it what?" Molly whispered.

"You don't think it's one of those rogue cowboys the grown-ups were talking about at breakfast, do you?" Finn asked.

"I don't think rogue cowboys live in tree branches," Molly said.

"They don't," Ella said. "I told you, the rogue cowboys don't really exist. The sound is just a family of woodpeckers."

"Woodpeckers!" Molly exclaimed. "I've never seen one in person!"

But when she looked up, all she could see were rustling leaves in the branches of the towering birch trees.

Roger circled back to check on the kids.

"Thanks for helping our new buckaroos, Ella. Now, kids, look over yonder, about two miles as the crow flies," he said. "That's the Blue River, which flows into the great Colorado River. And see that, way up over there?"

"Oh wow," Finn said. "Is that Mount Everest?"

Molly giggled. "Mount Everest isn't in Colorado," she said. "It's not even in the United States."

"That's Mount Lincoln, right, Dad?" Ella asked.

"Right you are, young lady," Roger said proudly.

"Well, it could've been Mount Everest," Finn muttered. "It looks like the biggest mountain in the world."

"It's not even the biggest mountain in the

Rocky Mountains," Roger told him. "That'd be Mount Elbert. We're a few days away from that sight. For now, we're going to set up camp just ahead of that clearing."

"Whoa," Molly said. "A few *days?*"

She looked over at Finn, knowing he was thinking the same thing she was: How long was this work in Colorado going to take?

"Look over there!" Roger said. "There's a gang of elk!" Then he gave his horse a kick to return to the front of the herd.

The kids looked toward the elk. They were huge, deerlike animals with tall antlers coming out of their heads.

"There are a lot of elk in these mountains," Ella said. "The moose are a little shyer, but sometimes you get to see them, too."

They kept riding. They didn't see any

moose, or any more elk for that matter—though they did see two prairie dogs, three rabbits, and best of all, a bald eagle soaring overhead.

Finally, they reached the clearing where Roger said they were to set up camp. Finn climbed down off Rocket. Then Finn and Ella helped Molly carefully get down from Dasha. The adults busied themselves hammering stakes into the ground, stretching out tents, and gathering the wood and water they'd need for the night.

"Did you hear that?" Finn asked.

"Another woodpecker?" Molly guessed.

"I don't think so," Ella said. "It sounds like horses."

Suddenly, the camp was filled with the thundering sound of horse hooves crashing through the woods. Three cowboys with red bandannas tied around their mouths and big brown cowboy hats shading their faces rode through the clearing. Their horses kicked up giant clouds of dust. They galloped out to the pasture of grazing animals. Their white horses slowed down for a split second, and then the cowboys took off back into the woods as fast as they arrived. The white cows with black splotches, the brown cows with white patches, the big cows, and the baby cows were all mooing in confusion and concern.

And Snowflake . . .

Wait! Where was Snowflake?

The most famous cow in Colorado was gone.

Chapter Eight
FOLLOW THAT COW!

"The rogue cowboys!" Molly whispered. "Do you think they took Snowflake?"

Ella and Finn were too shocked to respond.

"How did this happen?" Roger yelled at Snowflake's bodyguards.

"You asked us for help with the bedrolls," one of the bodyguards said. "We can't watch the cow and help you at the same time."

"I didn't think you'd *both* turn your backs on Snowflake," Roger said.

"Do you think it was the EZ Cheezys who took the cow, Dad?" Ella asked.

"No doubt about it," Roger said.

"Who are the EZ Cheezys?" Finn asked.

"Remember what Cliff said? They're the people who want to hook Snowflake up to machines," Molly said. "They want her milk so they can make cheese and sell it."

"Oh, right," Finn said.

"What if we never see Snowflake again?" Ella said.

"They'll have to change the name of the ranch," Finn said. "They can't have a Snowflake Ranch with no Snowflake."

Ella looked like she was about to cry.

"Sure they can," Molly told him. "They can

call the ranch whatever they want. They can call it the Brontosaurus Ranch, even though there aren't any dinosaurs." She paused, and then added, "But it may be too sad to look at all those T-shirts and mugs with white cows on them, knowing Snowflake is gone."

"We need a plan," Roger said. "First, we'll cut this trip short. Inexperienced ranchers should head back to the Snowflake Ranch and—"

"Now hang on," someone said. It was the man from breakfast. He was in his new flannel shirt—the one that Finn saved from a ketchup spill. "We paid good money for a real cattle drive experience, and I'm not turning back just a day into the trip."

"We can help find those rogue cowboys," the man in the green button-down offered.

"No, it's too dangerous," a woman said.

"Who cares about a stinkin' cow anyway?" another man asked.

The group gasped.

"What? Cows are a dime a dozen out here," he said. "We can continue on without her, right?"

"We cannot continue without Snowflake," Roger said.

The grown-ups kept arguing. Nobody could agree on a plan.

"This is terrible," Ella said. "The longer they fight, the more time passes. And the more time passes, the farther away those guys are taking Snowflake."

"Ella, listen," Molly said. "How well do you know these trails?"

"Pretty well," Ella said. "I've ridden them every summer of my whole life."

"Good," Molly said. "We're going to look for Snowflake ourselves."

"We are?" Finn asked.

"That's right," said Molly. "We have work to do."

"And if we find her, what do we do? It's not like the three of us are any match for those cowboys," said Ella.

"We're not going to fight them," Molly said. "We're going to trick them. I'll tell them I'm lost and looking for my parents. I'll be really upset and even pretend to cry. I'm really good at that. When I was in the school play this spring, I read a whole acting book on how to make yourself cry."

"You did? But you were a tree!" Finn said.

Molly shrugged. "What can I say, I like to be prepared. The book said if you want to cry, either you have to get into the character's head or, if you can't do that, think of something that makes you really sad."

"So you can cry. Then what happens?" Finn asked.

"Then they'll turn around to look at me, and their backs will be to Snowflake. That's when you two come in," Molly continued. "You'll be watching from behind a tree or a rock, and you'll move in as fast as you can, grab Snowflake, and lead her back to camp."

"Wait a second," Ella said. "What about *you?* The cowboys are going to notice Snowflake is gone, and what if they blame you? There's three of them and one of you. Plus, they're big and you're little. They'll catch you for sure."

"Yeah, and Mom and Dad will freak out

if you're captured by rogue cowboys," Finn said.

"Unless . . . ," Ella said.

"Unless what?" Molly asked.

"Unless we set booby traps," Ella said.

"Do you know how to make them?" Finn asked.

"Course I do," Ella said. "My dad taught me. All we need are some logs and rope."

Finn turned to his sister. "I'm not sure about this. I think the grown-ups—"

"The grown-ups are fighting too much to come up with a plan," Molly said.

"You heard them," Ella added.

"I guess you're right," Finn said. "Let's get to work!"

Chapter Nine
ROGUE COWBOYS

Molly, Finn, and Ella rode out of the camp and into the woods while the grown-ups continued to argue. Ella spotted four sets of hoof tracks—three for the cowboys' horses and one for poor Snowflake. The kids followed them across a field to a tree-lined trail, beside a gurgling brook, and eventually down a narrow pathway shaded by tall spruce trees.

"We need to be on the lookout for small

logs," Ella said as they rode their horses single file. "If you see a good one, let me know. We can string it up between two of these spruces."

"If we ever find Snowflake," Finn said. "It's too muddy here. I don't even see the tracks anymore."

"Look, there's a clearing up ahead!" Ella said. "I bet they went that way!" She gave her horse a kick, and then Finn did, too.

"Oh brother," Molly said. But this whole rescue mission was her idea. She tightened her grip on the reins and gave Dasha a little nudge with the heel of her boot. They followed Ella and Finn toward the clearing.

They all rode down a rocky path that led into a big open field filled with clover. Snowflake was all the way across the meadow. Alone.

"There she is!" Molly cried.

"Let's go," Finn said.

"Wait! We have to set the booby traps," Ella reminded them.

The kids dismounted their horses. Ella had a lasso, so they used that to string up a couple of logs—perfect booby traps for Molly to duck under, when the time came to run away.

They were all set. Molly was ready to walk up to the cowboys and cry. She wasn't playing a character, so she had to think of something sad from her own life. What made Molly sad? She got one question wrong on her spelling test. But she wasn't really sad about that. And she hadn't gotten what she wanted for her birthday. She wasn't really sad about that, either. Just disappointed.

Molly fingered her friendship bracelet,

thinking. Her friendship bracelet! She had no one to give it to. Now, that was sad! Molly felt tears start to form. She tiptoed forward and then—

"OW!" Molly cried.

"What happened?" Ella asked, her voice just above a whisper.

"I stubbed my toe on a tree root," Molly whispered back.

"Shh," Finn said. "Molly, you should—"

But before he could finish his sentence, there was a whooshing sound. A cowboy's lasso fell around their shoulders. They were trapped!

"Got 'em!" one of the rogue cowboys cried.

He pulled them in closer. The kids kicked and screamed and tried to get loose. But it was no use. The lasso held them tight.

"Let's see what we've got here, Chuck," another one said. "Hey, I recognize these kids. They were with that Snowflake Ranch group."

"Ah, how cute that they'd think they could come in here and get their cow back," said Chuck. "That's what you're here for, aren't you?"

Ella spit dirt out of her mouth. "Yes!" she said. "It's not right for you to take something that doesn't belong to you!"

The cowboys threw their heads back and laughed.

"What should we do with them, Butch?" Chuck asked.

"They're too skinny to eat," Butch said.

"You'd *eat* us?" Finn asked. His eyes widened in surprise.

The rogue cowboys ignored him. "Should we bring them back to EZ Cheezy and let the Cheez-master deal with them?" the third cowboy asked.

"Nah. Let's just tie 'em to a tree and leave 'em," Chuck said.

"But we'll starve to death!" Molly cried.

The cowboys laughed again. Chuck dragged the kids back toward the line of trees. "Look at these," he said to his fellow cowboys. "Booby traps." He slipped a pocketknife through Ella's lasso, and the log fell to the ground. "Where'd you learn to make these?" he asked the kids. "Preschool for cowboys?"

"We're goners," Finn whispered to his sister. "When I woke up this morning, I didn't expect to die in Colorado."

"Hey, Chuck," the third cowboy said, "maybe we should let them go. They're just little kids."

"They found us once; they could find us again," Butch said.

"Yeah," Chuck agreed. "This cow is going to make us a fortune. Don't throw away your millions saving these little weasels, Doc."

Doc shook his head. He used his own lasso to help tie Ella, Molly, and Finn to the spruce. Across the clearing, Snowflake was eating grass, unaware that the kids had risked their lives to save her—and that they had failed.

"You're not going to get away with this," Ella said in a brave voice. "I'm sure my dad is already looking for us."

"Our parents, too. They probably called the police!" Molly said. She hoped the men couldn't tell that she was lying. She only lied in an emergency, and it might not even be a lie. If her parents had discovered she and Finn were missing, they would've made that call for sure.

"You think there are police out here who will come to rescue you?" Chuck asked. "That's cute."

"Let's get going," Butch said.

"Just a sec," Doc said. "I want to tie them supertight."

Finn had an itch on his back. Just his luck. He was tied up, and the itch was driving him crazy. Then he had an idea. An idea that was so unusual it just might work.

"Stop squirming!" Doc said.

But Finn didn't listen. He fidgeted and moved his body against the scratchy bark of the trunk, using the tree as a back scratcher.

Suddenly, there was the shriek of sirens.

Doc jumped in surprise.

"We told you our parents called the police!" Finn said.

The cowboys scrambled to get on their horses. "Forget these kids, let's get out of here," Chuck yelled.

They left in a cloud of dust. Snowflake was still grazing in the field.

"Where are the police?" Ella asked.

"No police," Finn said. "It's my baseball video game. I remembered it was in my pocket. I figured that if I could get it turned on, the sound would scare those guys."

"Wow," Ella said. "You don't have anything in your pocket that could untie us, do you?"

"No, sorry," Finn said.

"What should we do now?" Molly asked.

"Let's scream and hope my dad is looking for us, and that he hears us," Ella said.

So that's what they did. They yelled louder and longer than they ever had in their lives. All the while, Snowflake lazily ate grass. Finally, they heard voices in the distance. "We're over here!" the kids cried. "Help!"

Roger rode up and quickly untied the kids from their tree. He gave Ella a big hug.

"Dad, we saved Snowflake!" Ella cried.

"But the rogue cowboys got away," Molly said.

"No, they didn't," Roger said. "We found them. Turns out your old dad is good with a lasso, Ella. We tied them together, and we're waiting for help to arrive."

"Phew," said Finn.

"Nice job, ranchers," Roger said, tipping his hat. "Thanks to your help, Snowflake is safe. But I don't want you ever wandering off without a grown-up again."

"We won't," the kids promised.

"All's well that ends well," Roger said. "You did good work today."

Work! Finn and Molly looked at each other with wide eyes and raised eyebrows. They half expected PET to show up right then.

But it didn't.

"Y'all follow me now," Roger said. "You've earned yourself a celebration!"

Chapter Ten

SWING YOUR PARTNER

After a few more miles on the trail, they finally arrived at a clearing with picnic tables and— "Is that a dance floor?" Molly asked.

"What's a dance floor doing in the middle of Colorado?" Finn asked.

"You'll see," Ella told them.

Helen was straightening trays of food on the tables. She walked over to Finn and Molly as the group rode up. She offered a hand to help the twins off their horses, but they were able to dismount on their own.

"Impressive," she said. "I can see that you've learned a lot on your travels. Help yourself to fresh lemonade and treats."

"How'd you get here so fast?" Molly asked her.

"Cliff and I rode without cows," Helen explained. "It went much faster."

The sound of music filled the air, and the kids' heads swiveled toward a group of musicians at the edge of the clearing. They were wearing matching plaid shirts and playing fiddles and banjos.

"The band is doing a sound check," Helen explained. "They're almost warmed up!"

Ella, Molly, and Finn headed toward a table covered in a blue-and-white-checkered tablecloth. They poured glasses of lemonade and ate cheese sticks, mac and cheese, and miniature grilled cheese sandwiches, and they dunked pieces of bread and apples into a towering fountain of melted cheese. It was all made from Snowflake's prized milk, and every bite tasted better than the last. The cheese was creamy and sweet with the slightest hint of clover. No wonder those EZ Cheezys wanted to steal Snowflake!

"Welcome, ranchers!" a voice boomed. "Let's get this party started!"

Ella clapped her hands together excitedly. "It's time for the square dance!" she cried. "The state dance of Colorado!"

"Colorado has a state dance?" Molly asked. "I didn't know there was such a thing as state dances!"

"Looks like you don't know everything about the United States," Finn said.

"You're right," Molly said. She offered Finn a small smile. "I'm sorry I can be such a know-it-all."

"You *do* know an awful lot about geography," Finn said.

"But you knew how to scare off those rogue cowboys," Molly said. "That was really smart."

"Thanks," Finn said.

"Plus, you know a lot about baseball," she told him. "I'll never give you a hard time about your game again."

"Can I get that in writing?" Finn asked.

"You wish," Molly said with a grin. She pushed her brother's baseball cap down over his eyes.

Finn straightened his cap.

"Come on," Ella called. "Let's go!"

The kids ran to the dance floor. Helen explained that everyone had to stand in a square—four pairs per square. Helen and Cliff, Roger and Ella, Finn and Molly, and the man with the green shirt and his wife stood together.

"Now, we'll start with a little do-si-do," Helen said. "Ladies, stand at your partner's right shoulder. He'll circle around you. Then, gents, step back and let the ladies do the same."

"I have a question," Molly said, and Helen nodded for her to ask. "I get to keep my feet on the ground the whole time, right?"

"You sure do," Helen said, laughing. "I promise."

Molly glanced at her boots. "I'm still not sure about this," she said.

"The caller will tell you what to do," Helen assured her, nodding toward one of the guys in the band.

The music started up. "Bow to your partner. Bow to the corner. Wave to the folks across the square."

Finn and Molly and all the others bowed and waved. Finn circled Molly, and Molly circled him. Before they knew it, they were do-si-do-ing, flutterwheeling, and a whole lot more.

98

Roger smiled at the kids, which made Finn and Molly feel slightly homesick for their own mom and dad.

But there wasn't any time to think too hard about that, because the bandleader was shouting more instructions.

"All join hands and circle to the right, circle to the left!"

"Now promenade the square!"

Finn was a natural. He didn't mess up any of the steps. It looked like he had been square dancing all his life. Molly did her best.

"Swing your partner round and round, swing 'em all around the town!"

"I'm so dizzy," Molly said, knocking into Ella. "But this is really fun."

"One last do-si-do!"

"We have to square dance back in Ohio," Finn said.

After a while, the band announced it would be taking a quick break. The kids went to get lemonade refills.

"You guys are good for first timers," Ella said. "I'm so glad you came to the Snowflake Ranch!"

Just then, Finn and Molly heard a faint honk in the distance. *PET?*

"And we're back!" the bandleader called. "Grab your partner!" The banjo music started up again.

"Oh yay, it's time to dance!" Ella leapt to her feet.

Molly fingered her friendship bracelet. "Wait, Ella. I want to give you something first. It's a friendship bracelet." She took it off her wrist and put it on Ella's. "Now, we can be friends no matter what state we're in."

"Thanks, Molly!" Ella said. "I love it! It fits perfectly!"

"If you're ever in Ohio, you should come to a baseball game with us," Finn said. "There are the Cincinnati Reds, the Cleveland Indians, and the Ohio State Buckeyes. Or you could come to one of my Little League games." He looked down so she wouldn't see him blush.

"That would be awesome," Ella replied. "Come on, let's go dance!"

She turned back to the dance floor. But the twins knew what they had to do. They joined hands and ran across the field.

Chapter Eleven
HOME, SWEET HOME

PET was parked in the grass on the other side of the trees. It was as if the camper had been waiting for them all along. The screen was lit up when the twins climbed in. "Fasten your seat belts, kids," PET said. "We're leaving in three, two—"

"Wait!" Finn said, fumbling with his seat belt.

The instant it clicked, the camper took

off. The mountains, the prairies, and the rivers flew by the windows in a blur.

"We're headed home, right?" Molly asked.

Before PET answered, it stopped with a jolt. Out the windows, the twins could see their white house, the hunter-green mailbox, and the Johnny-jump-ups in the window boxes. Their home at 24 Birchwood Drive had never looked so good.

"My work here is done," PET said, and it went dark once again.

"Holy guacamole!" Finn said. "Can you believe that happened?"

"No, I can't," said Molly. "But we don't have time to talk about it now. We have to let Mom and Dad know we're home safe!"

She and Finn unbuckled their seat belts and headed for the door. Out of the corner of his eye, Finn spotted the map of the world, with its one lone pushpin stuck in Harvey Falls, Ohio. "Hang on," he told his sister. He picked up a blue pushpin and stuck it smack in the center of Colorado. "All right, let's go."

They ran into the house, calling, "Mom! Dad! We're here!"

Mrs. Parker walked into the foyer. She was

wearing a sundress. She looked very relaxed for someone whose kids had been missing for a whole day.

"There's no need to shout," she told the twins. "Are you hungry?"

Finn and Molly looked at each other, knowing they were thinking the same exact thing. They both shrugged. "Sure, I guess."

"Well, good. Your dad says omelets will be ready in five."

They walked into the kitchen, their legs feeling funny. Almost like they were still riding horses.

Mr. Parker was at the stove, adding diced ham and peppers to the pan. "Well, hello, sleepyheads!" he said, turning around to greet them. "We thought you'd never wake up!"

"But, Dad, we've been up for hours," Molly said. "Look at—"

She stopped herself. She was about to say "Look at our clothes." But when she looked at Finn, she realized that they were no longer dressed for a cattle drive. Finn was wearing his pajamas, and she was back in her leggings and fuzzy bunny slippers. When had she changed out of her gingham shirt and jeans? What happened to their boots and her cowboy hat?

"Take a seat," her father said. "Denver omelets coming right up."

Molly and Finn shared a startled look. *Did he just say 'Denver'? As in the capital of Colorado?*

They sat down at the table.

"We need to eat fast," Mr. Parker said. "We don't want to be late for the game."

"But my game is on Saturday," Finn said.

"Every week," Mr. Parker said. "We have to get a move on."

"Wait a sec," Molly said. "What day is it today?"

"Saturday, silly," their dad replied. "Yesterday was Friday and school ended. Have you forgotten your days of the week already?"

The twins looked at each other, and without speaking, they knew that they were thinking the same thing: it had been a dream, after all.

Mr. Parker set plates in front of Molly and Finn, and they all sat down for their normal Saturday breakfast.

Mrs. Parker added a splash of milk to her

mug of coffee. But before she took a sip, she paused to pick a piece of yellow hay from Molly's hair. "It looks like you've been rolling around a barn in your sleep."

Molly looked at Finn, then back at her parents. "Hey, Dad, about that camper..."

Colorado State Facts

- The Rocky Mountains run along the western border of Colorado.

- The Colorado state tree is the blue spruce. The state flower is the *Aquilegia caerulea*, also known as the white and lavender columbine, and the state bird is the lark bunting.

- The Colorado state flag looks like this:

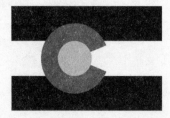

- Colorado is bordered by Wyoming, Nebraska, Kansas, Oklahoma, New Mexico, and Utah.

- The southwest point of Colorado touches the corners of Arizona's, New Mexico's, and Utah's borders. It's the only place in America where the corners of four states meet.

- Denver is the state capital.

- The Blue River is a tributary of the Colorado River.

- Mount Lincoln is the eighth-highest point in the Rocky Mountains.

- Mount Elbert is the highest point in the Rocky Mountains.

PET's favorite Colorado fact:

- Rumor has it that millions of dollars' worth of treasure is buried somewhere in the Rocky Mountains. . . . Maybe Molly's and Finn's horses galloped right past it!

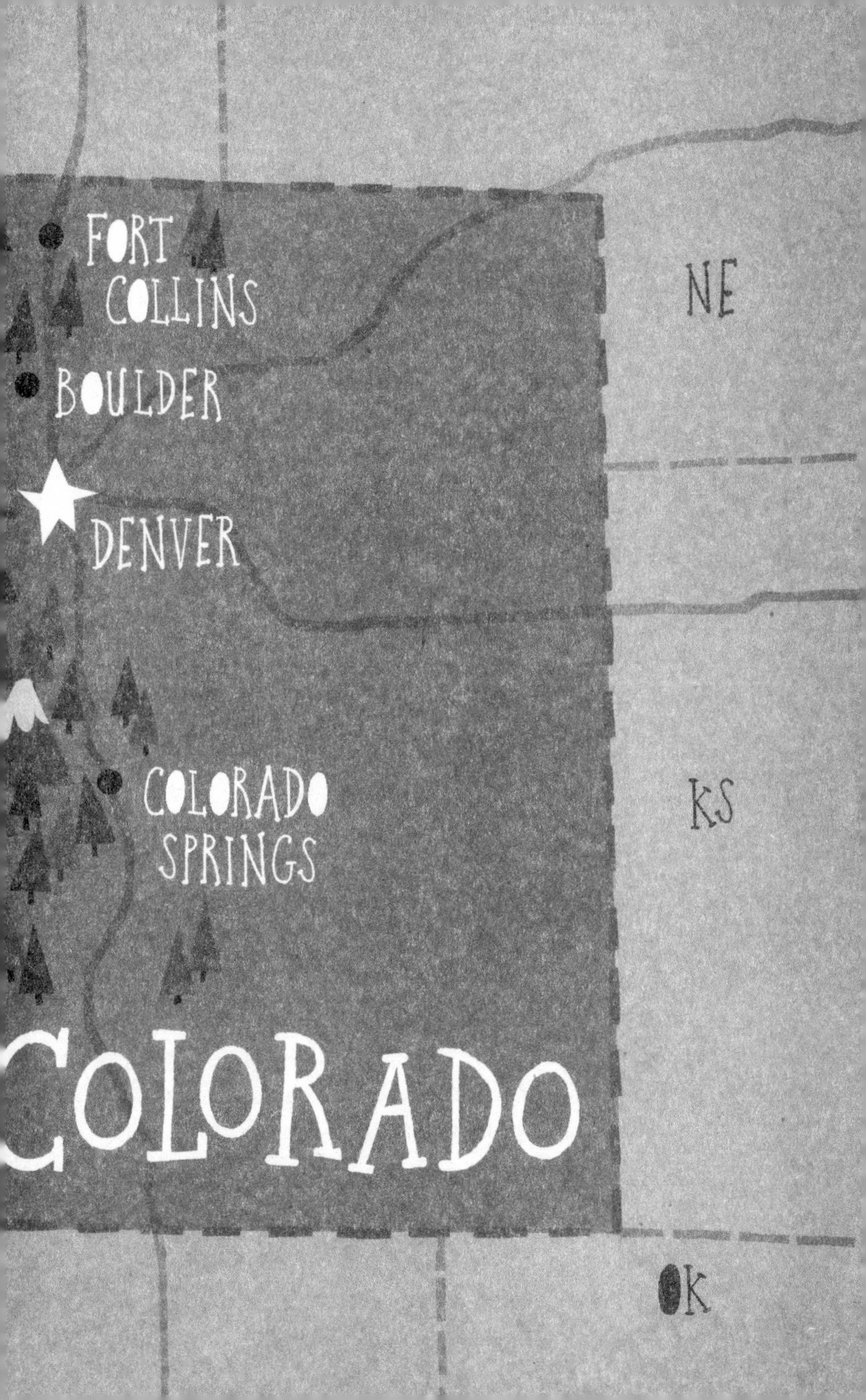
FORT COLLINS
BOULDER
DENVER
COLORADO SPRINGS
COLORADO
NE
KS
OK

Finn and Molly's work here is done,
but the adventures are just beginning!

Don't miss their next mission!

MAGIC ON THE MAP ②

THE SHOW MUST GO ON

PET's dashboard screen lit up in every color of the rainbow. Molly and Finn grabbed on to their armrests tightly. Even when you're excited about something, you can still be afraid. The camper started to hum, then it started to shake. There was a near-blinding flash of white light, and they were off!

Molly squeezed her eyes shut, but she

opened them when Finn called out. "Hey! Look!"

A flock of birds with royal-blue and reddish-brown feathers flew by the windshield. "Oh, those are eastern bluebirds," Molly said. "Aren't they beautiful?"

They sailed over a trio of waterfalls, fields of green, and trees. . . .

"I think those are apple trees!" Molly cried.

"Look over there! Is that the ocean?" Finn asked.

"Wow, I think so!"

"Cool!"

But pretty soon the ocean wasn't in sight anymore. All they saw were buildings, and more buildings, and even more buildings. And then the camper landed with a jolt.

Molly knew exactly what PET was going to say even before it said, "I'll be back when your work here is done." With that, the screen went blank. The camper doors swung open. Molly and Finn quickly undid their seat belts and jumped down onto the asphalt.

"Where are we?" Finn asked.

Molly looked around. They were standing in an alley, in the shadow of tall buildings. In the distance, there were muffled sounds of tires screeching and horns honking. When Molly turned toward the camper again, it had disappeared.

She looked over at Finn. "Uh, Finn," she started. "You're not going to like this."

She pointed to something on her brother's shirt.

Finn felt his heart beat a little faster as he

looked down. Gone were his plaid pajamas. In their place were blue jeans and a white-and-navy-pinstripe baseball jersey.

"Are you okay?" Molly asked.

"I'm a traitor is what I am," Finn said. He turned around. "What's on my back?"

"The number two," Molly said. "And then over that it says 'Jeter.'"

"Ugh," Finn said. "Jeter. One of the best shortstops in history and a five-time World Series champion. He played twenty years—for the Yankees!"

"The Yankees?" Molly asked. She'd heard that team name before. Finn had definitely talked about them. They were a good team . . . but where were they from?

Can you guess where
Finn and Molly are?

Answer: New York.

Travel with Finn and Molly in the

MAGIC ON THE MAP books!

Have you read them all?